STARK LIBRARY SEP - - 2022

CHECKERBOARD BIOGRAPHIES

TOM BRADY

JESSICA RUSICK

Checkerboard Library

An Imprint of Abdo Publishing
abdobooks.com

ABDOBOOKS.COM

Published by Abdo Publishing, a division of ABDO, PO Box 398166, Minneapolis, Minnesota 55439. Copyright © 2022 by Abdo Consulting Group, Inc. International copyrights reserved in all countries. No part of this book may be reproduced in any form without written permission from the publisher. Checkerboard Library™ is a trademark and logo of Abdo Publishing.

Printed in the United States of America, North Mankato, Minnesota
052021
092021

THIS BOOK CONTAINS RECYCLED MATERIALS

Design and Production: Mighty Media, Inc.
Editor: Liz Salzmann
Cover Photograph: Icon Sportswire/Getty Images
Interior Photographs: All-Pro Reels/Wikimedia Commons, pp. 13, 28 (bottom); Ashley Landis/AP Images, pp. 25, 29 (bottom); Ben Liebenberg/AP Images, pp. 5, 29 (top right); Charlie Riedel/AP Images, p. 27; Jallen8307/Wikimedia Commons, p. 9; JEFF ROBERSON/AP Images, p. 15; Keith Allison/Wikimedia Commons, p. 21; MGoBlog-Bryan Fuller/Flickr, p. 11; Shutterstock Images, pp. 17, 19 (paper clip), 29; Tony Tomsic/AP Images, p. 7; Wikimedia Commons, pp. 19, 23, 28

Library of Congress Control Number: 2021932877

Publisher's Cataloging-in-Publication Data
Names: Rusick, Jessica, author.
Title: Tom Brady / by Jessica Rusick
Description: Minneapolis, Minnesota : Abdo Publishing, 2022 | Series: Checkerboard biographies | Includes online resources and index.
Identifiers: ISBN 9781532195976 (lib. bdg.) | ISBN 9781098216832 (ebook)
Subjects: LCSH: Brady, Thomas Edward, Jr., 1977- --Juvenile literature. | Quarterbacks (Football)--United States--Biography--Juvenile literature. | Professional athletes--United States--Biography--Juvenile literature. | Tampa Bay Buccaneers (Football team)--Juvenile literature. | Super Bowl--Records--Juvenile literature.
Classification: DDC 796.332092--dc23

CONTENTS

ALL-STAR ATHLETE 4

YOUNG SPORTS STAR 6

TWO-SPORT TALENT 8

COLLEGE QUARTERBACK 10

PATRIOTS PLAYER 12

SUPER BOWL SUCCESSES 14

UPS AND DOWNS 16

SUCCESS AND SCANDAL 20

SUPER BOWL STAR 22

FOREVER A LEGEND 24

TIMELINE 28

GLOSSARY 30

ONLINE RESOURCES 31

INDEX 32

CHAPTER 1

ALL-STAR ATHLETE

Tom Brady is a National Football League (NFL) quarterback. He is considered by many to be the greatest quarterback of all time. He has won seven Super Bowl championships. Brady has also been named the NFL's Most Valuable Player (MVP) in the Super Bowl five times. In addition to these achievements, Brady is known for his leadership and determination.

Brady joined the NFL in 2000 as a backup quarterback for the New England Patriots. In 2001, he became starting quarterback. That season, Brady led the Patriots to a Super Bowl victory. He went on to be the team's star quarterback for the next 18 years.

In 2020, Brady joined the Tampa Bay Buccaneers. Many people wondered if he could win a Super Bowl with a different team. That season, Brady proved that he could, leading the team to a win over the Kansas City Chiefs.

Brady holds the Vince Lombardi trophy following his team's Super Bowl win in 2021. The Super Bowl trophy is named after a former NFL coach.

CHAPTER 2

YOUNG SPORTS STAR

Thomas Edward Patrick Brady Jr. was born on **August 3, 1977, in San Mateo, California.** His family called him Tommy. Tommy's father, Tom Sr., worked for an insurance company. Tommy's mother, Galynn, was a flight attendant. Tommy grew up with three older sisters. They are Maureen, Nancy, and Julie.

Sports were an important part of Tommy's childhood. Tommy, his parents, and his sisters were all huge sports fans. Tommy played soccer, basketball, baseball, and flag football. His sisters played softball and soccer. Tommy often cheered his sisters on while they played.

The Brady family frequently went to San Francisco 49ers football games together. There, Tommy watched famed 49ers quarterback Joe Montana play. Montana is considered one of the greatest football players of all time. He was Tommy's hero. In the future, Tommy hoped to be a football star just like Montana.

Montana played for the 49ers from 1979 to 1992. He led the team to four Super Bowl championships.

CHAPTER 3

TWO-SPORT TALENT

In 1991, Brady began attending Junipero Serra High School in San Mateo. There, he played both football and baseball. As a **freshman**, Brady was backup quarterback on the junior **varsity** football team. Brady rarely played. But he trained hard, staying late after practices to work on his skills. In his **sophomore** year, Brady started as quarterback for the first time. His extra training paid off. That year, Brady led his team to the championship game!

Brady was starting quarterback for the school's varsity team his junior and senior years. He hoped to earn a **scholarship** to play football in college. So, Brady and his father sent **highlight reels** of Brady's football games to college football coaches across the country. Brady's athleticism and ability to throw the ball impressed several coaches.

Meanwhile, Brady was also getting noticed for his baseball skills. Brady was the catcher on his school's varsity baseball team. Many baseball **scouts** believed he could play professionally. After Brady graduated,

In 2012, Junipero Serra High School named its football stadium Brady Family Stadium in Brady's honor.

he was **drafted** by the Montreal Expos, a Major League Baseball team.

However, that year Brady had also accepted a **scholarship** to play football at the University of Michigan. He enjoyed football more than baseball. So in fall 1995, Brady went to Ann Arbor, Michigan, to begin his college career.

CHAPTER 4

COLLEGE QUARTERBACK

During Brady's first year at Michigan, he was a redshirt athlete on the Wolverines football team. This means he trained with the team but did not play in any games. In 1996 and 1997, Brady was one of several backup quarterbacks. So, he did not play much. But he worked hard to prove that he deserved more time on the field.

Brady earned the starting quarterback position in 1998 and 1999. Over these two seasons, he had a 20-5 record and threw 35 touchdowns. Brady graduated from the University of Michigan in December 1999 with a degree in general studies. In January 2000, he led the team to victory in the Orange Bowl. This was Brady's final game as a Wolverine.

Brady wanted to go on to play football in the NFL. Each spring, the NFL holds a **draft** to acquire new

> **Always know that you're an active participant in your life. Your life will be what you make of it.**

In 2016, Brady returned to Michigan for the Wolverine's game against the University of Colorado. He met with the team before the game and served as honorary captain.

players. Most of the players are recent college graduates. The **draft** has seven rounds. During each round, teams take turns picking players they want.

In April 2000, Brady entered the NFL draft. He believed he would be picked early. But as the draft went on, Brady became unsure he would get picked at all. Waiting made Brady nervous. But finally, in the sixth round, he was drafted by the New England Patriots. Brady was relieved and excited.

CHAPTER 5

PATRIOTS PLAYER

Brady began his first season with the Patriots in fall 2000. He was one of several backup quarterbacks. The starting quarterback was Drew Bledsoe. Brady played in just one game during the season. In the meantime, he worked to build his strength and improve his skills. Brady hoped this would help earn him more playing time in the future.

The following season, Bledsoe was seriously injured during a game. Patriots coach Bill Belichick chose Brady to fill in. On September 30, 2001, Brady played his first full game as Patriots starting quarterback. During the game, Brady threw for 168 yards, helping the Patriots beat the Indianapolis Colts 44-13.

Bledsoe returned in November. But Belichick had been impressed by Brady's ability to lead the Patriots. So, he named Brady starter for the rest of the season. The Patriots won 11 out of the 14 games Brady started, earning a spot in the 2002 Super Bowl against the St. Louis Rams.

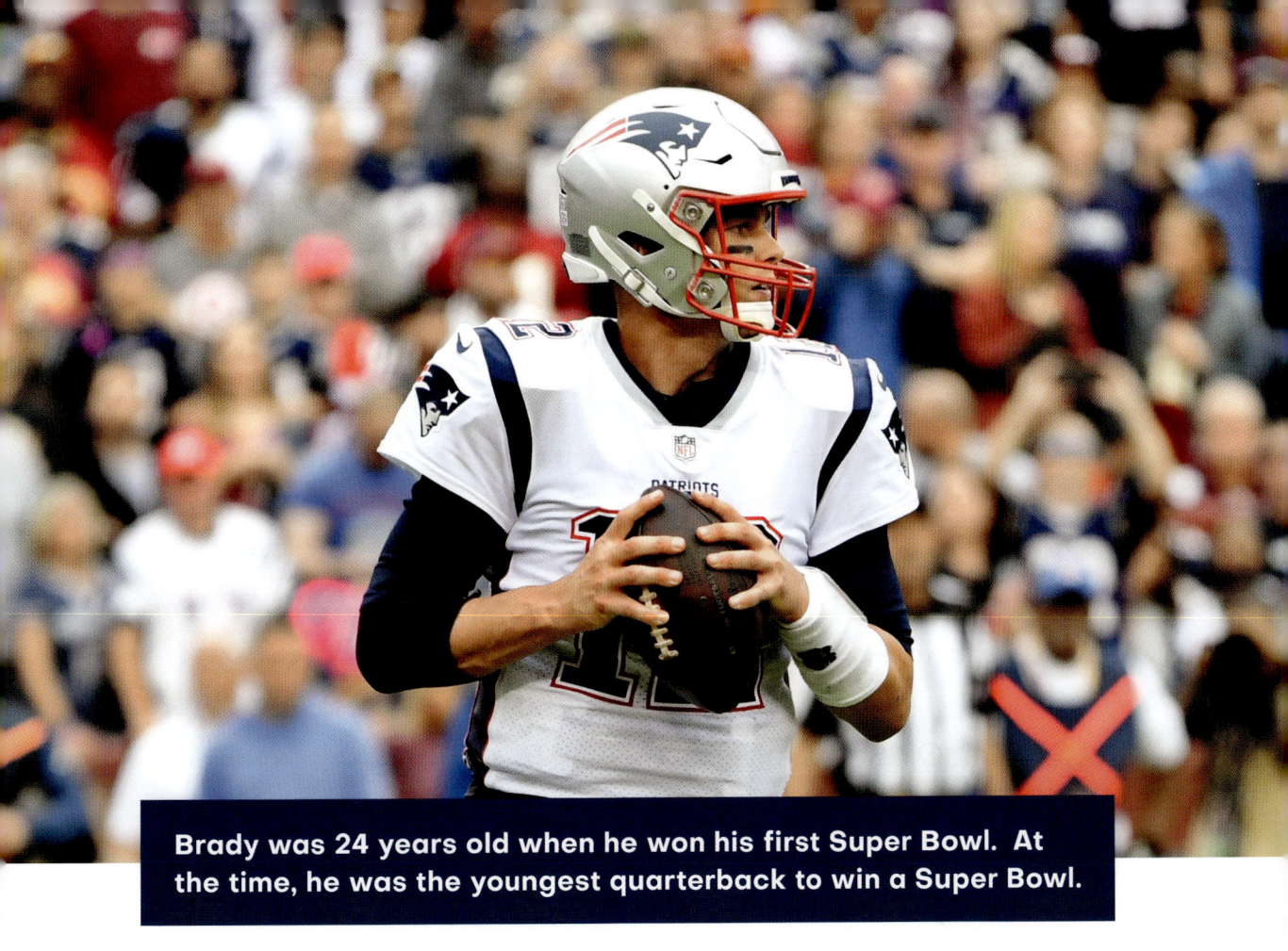

Brady was 24 years old when he won his first Super Bowl. At the time, he was the youngest quarterback to win a Super Bowl.

   Most people expected the Rams to win. But Brady and the Patriots played well. In the tied game's final minutes, Brady expertly moved the ball down the field. This put the Patriots in range to score the game-winning field goal. Brady had helped the Patriots win their first ever Super Bowl! He was named the game's MVP.

CHAPTER 6

SUPER BOWL SUCCESSES

With the Super Bowl win, Brady had solidified his place as the Patriots' starting quarterback. During the 2002 season, Brady led the league in touchdown passes. Although the Patriots finished the season with a 9–7 record, they did not make the playoffs.

After losing two of the first four games in 2003, the Patriots came back strong. Brady led the team on a 12-game winning streak for a 14–2 season overall. This was the best record in the league.

Following their record season, the Patriots once again made it to the Super Bowl. Brady threw for 354 yards and 3 touchdowns, helping beat the Carolina Panthers 32–29. During the game, Brady also set a record for most completed passes in a Super Bowl. And, he earned his second Super Bowl MVP award.

Brady continued to have success the following year. The Patriots returned to the Super Bowl in 2005, where they beat the Philadelphia Eagles. Brady had helped

Wide receiver Deion Branch was the MVP of the 2005 Super Bowl. He caught 11 passes from Brady during the game. At the time, this was a tie for the most receptions in a Super Bowl.

the Patriots win three Super Bowls in just four years. Thanks to Brady, the Patriots had become one of the NFL's best teams.

CHAPTER 7

UPS AND DOWNS

The Patriots returned to the playoffs in the 2005 and 2006 postseasons. However, they were unable to advance to the Super Bowl. Meanwhile, Brady had been dating actress Bridget Moynahan since 2004. They broke up in 2006. At the time, Bridget was **pregnant** with the couple's child. Their son John was born in August 2007. That same year, Brady began dating model Gisele Bündchen.

While his life changed off the field, Brady had an incredible season on the field. In 2007, he threw 50 regular season touchdown passes. At the time, this was the most of any quarterback in history. Brady also led the Patriots to a 16-0 season. This was only the second undefeated season in NFL history. Brady was named the NFL's regular season MVP.

The Patriots won two playoff games in the postseason. This meant the team would face the New York Giants in the Super Bowl. Many sports fans believed Brady and the Patriots were unstoppable. But the Giants played well, scoring a last-minute touchdown to win 17-14.

Brady and Bündchen at a gala at the Metropolitan Museum of Art in New York City

Sports writers called it one of the greatest upsets in Super Bowl history. In 2013, Brady said it had been the hardest loss of his career.

Brady's Super Bowl loss was followed by another difficult time. In the first game of the 2008 season, he suffered a serious knee injury. Brady could not play for the rest of the season while he recovered. Some wondered if the injury would end the star quarterback's career.

But Brady came back strong. In the 2009 season opener, he threw 378 yards and had two touchdowns against the Buffalo Bills. This helped the Patriots win the game. Later that season, he set a record for throwing five touchdowns in a single quarter.

The Patriots lost to the Baltimore Ravens in the 2009 playoffs. Brady was disappointed. However, he found his injury had given him a new attitude about playing. Even when his team lost, Brady now felt fortunate to walk off the field unhurt.

Brady also felt fortunate for his personal life. Brady and Bündchen married in 2009. The same year, their son Benjamin was born. In 2012, the couple welcomed a daughter, Vivian.

BIO BASICS

NAME: Thomas Edward Patrick Brady Jr.

NICKNAMES: Tom, Tommy

BIRTH: August 3, 1977, San Mateo, California

SPOUSE: Gisele Bündchen (2009-present)

CHILDREN: John, Benjamin, Vivian

FAMOUS FOR: his decades-long career as an NFL quarterback for the New England Patriots and Tampa Bay Buccaneers; being considered the greatest quarterback of all time

ACHIEVEMENTS: having the most Super Bowl wins and Super Bowl MVP Awards of any NFL player in history; being the oldest quarterback in history to start in and win a Super Bowl; having the most regular season and postseason wins of any quarterback in history

CHAPTER 8

SUCCESS AND SCANDAL

In 2011, Brady had another excellent season. He threw for the most passing yards of his career. The team made it to the Super Bowl but lost to the New York Giants.

Meanwhile, Brady focused on fitness. He followed a special diet and exercise plan to stay healthy. Brady wanted to help others stay healthy too. So, in 2013, he developed a health program called the TB12 Method.

In 2014, Brady continued to have success on the field. That season, he led the Patriots to another Super Bowl. However, Brady also faced a **scandal** known as "Deflategate." He was accused of having footballs **deflated** before a playoff game. This makes the balls easier to throw and catch. Brady denied any wrongdoing. But the Deflategate scandal dominated the news.

Brady tried not to think about the scandal as he prepared for the 2015 Super Bowl. During the game, Brady threw 37 completed passes, a Super Bowl record. This contributed to Brady's fourth Super Bowl win!

The name of Brady's TB12 Method is a combination of his initials and his jersey number.

CHAPTER 9

SUPER BOWL STAR

Brady **continued to succeed after his Super Bowl victory, leading the Patriots to the playoffs in 2015.** But in 2016, Brady was suspended for four games due to the 2014 Deflategate **scandal**. Brady still denied any wrongdoing. But, during his suspension, he was happy to spend extra time with his family.

Brady returned from his suspension as strong as ever. In December 2016, he earned his two hundred and first win as starting quarterback. This was the most of any quarterback in history.

That postseason, the Patriots faced the Atlanta Falcons in the 2017 Super Bowl. By the third quarter, the Patriots were down by 25 points. But Brady didn't give up. He passed for 466 yards during the game, a Super Bowl record. He also completed 43 passes, breaking his own record set in 2015. Brady's record-setting play helped the Patriots win 34-28 in overtime. It was the biggest comeback in Super Bowl history.

Brady also earned his fourth Super Bowl MVP award. This broke the record set by his childhood hero

During the 2017 Super Bowl, running back James White caught 14 of Brady's passes. This was a new record for receptions in a Super Bowl.

Joe Montana. In addition, Brady made history as the first quarterback to win five Super Bowl titles. Brady **dedicated** the win to his mother, who had battled and recovered from breast **cancer** during the 2016 season.

CHAPTER 10
FOREVER A LEGEND

After his 2017 Super Bowl win, Brady showed no signs of slowing down. The Patriots made it to the Super Bowl in 2018 and 2019. In 2018, they lost to the Philadelphia Eagles. But in 2019, the Patriots beat the Los Angeles Rams. This made Brady the oldest quarterback to win a Super Bowl. And, he now had six Super Bowl wins. This was more than any other player in history.

Brady wanted to remain with the Patriots after the 2019 season. But he and the team could not agree on a contract. So, Brady joined the Tampa Bay Buccaneers. Brady thanked Patriots fans for their support over the years. He said he would forever be a Patriot.

Brady was excited for a new opportunity in Tampa Bay. But the Buccaneers had not been to the playoffs since 2007. They had not won a playoff game since 2002. So, some people wondered whether Brady could lead the team to victory.

The year 2020 brought other challenges. The world was facing the **COVID-19 pandemic**. Brady's parents became sick with COVID-19, and his father was

One of Brady's best friends on the Patriots was tight end Rob Gronkowski (*left*). He retired in 2019. But when Brady joined the Buccaneers, Gronkowski came out of retirement to join his friend on the team!

hospitalized. Brady was stressed and worried about his parents. He called the hospital every day to talk to his father. Fortunately, his parents recovered.

Meanwhile, the Buccaneers kept winning. Brady led the team not only to the playoffs, but to the 2021 Super Bowl against the Kansas City Chiefs. The Chiefs were the reigning Super Bowl champions. The team was led by Patrick Mahomes, a talented quarterback nearly 20 years younger than Brady. Many sports experts expected the Chiefs to win.

But Brady once again proved his doubters wrong. He threw three touchdowns during the game, helping beat the Chiefs 31–9. It was Brady's seventh Super Bowl win. Brady also earned his fifth Super Bowl MVP award.

Sports fans wondered what was next for the star quarterback. Brady said he would continue to play in the 2021 regular season. After that, Brady believed he could play until his late 40s. No matter what Brady's future held, one thing was certain. Brady would forever be known as a football legend.

> **My favorite [Super Bowl] ring? I've always said the next one. The next one's the best.**

Brady celebrates with his children after winning the 2021 Super Bowl. Some people at the game wore face masks to protect themselves from COVID-19.

TIMELINE

1977
Tom Brady is born on August 3 in San Mateo, California.

2000
Brady is drafted by the New England Patriots.

2002
Brady leads the Patriots to the team's first Super Bowl win.

2007
In August, Brady's son John is born. Brady leads the Patriots to an undefeated regular season.

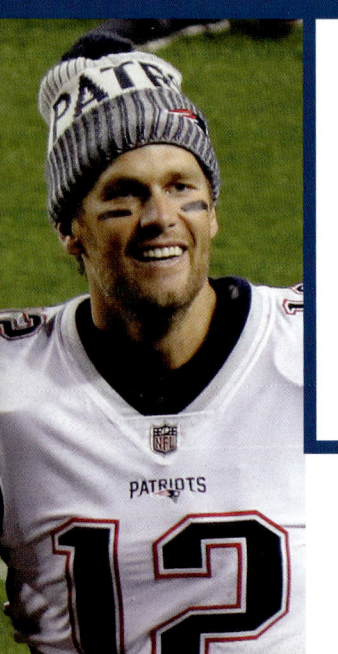

1995
Brady accepts a scholarship to play football for the University of Michigan.

2001
Brady becomes the Patriots starting quarterback.

2005
The Patriots win their third Super Bowl in four years.

2008
Brady misses most of the regular season following a knee injury.

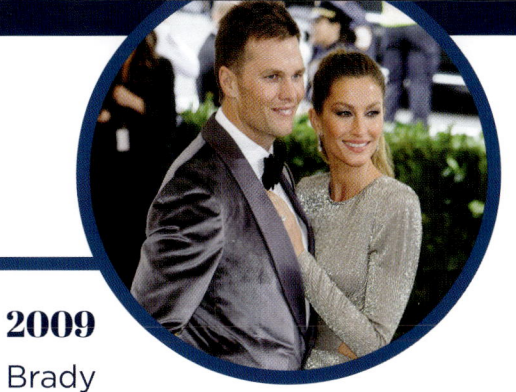

2009
Brady marries Gisele Bündchen. Their son, Benjamin, is born later that year.

2015
Brady earns his fourth Super Bowl win.

2019
Brady earns his sixth Super Bowl win, the most of any NFL player in history at the time.

2021
Brady wins his seventh Super Bowl title in the 2020 postseason and earns his fifth Super Bowl MVP award.

2012
Brady's daughter Vivian is born.

2017
Brady wins his fifth Super Bowl title after the Patriots make the biggest comeback in Super Bowl history.

2020
Brady leaves the Patriots and joins the Tampa Bay Buccaneers.

29

GLOSSARY

cancer—any of a group of often deadly diseases marked by harmful changes in the normal growth of cells. Cancer can spread and destroy healthy tissues and organs.

COVID-19—a serious illness that first appeared in late 2019.

dedicate—to say that a work, performance, or accomplishment was made in someone's honor.

deflate—to let the air or gas out of something.

draft—a system for or act of selecting individuals from a group. People may be drafted for required military service or sports teams.

freshman—of or related to the first year of high school or college.

highlight reel—a film or video that shows an athlete's abilities, skills, and accomplishments.

pandemic—an outbreak of a disease that spreads quickly throughout the world.

pregnant—having one or more babies growing within the body.

scandal—an action that shocks people and disgraces those connected with it.

scholarship—money or aid given to help a student continue his or her studies.

scout—a person who evaluates the talent of amateur athletes to determine if they would have success in the pros.

sophomore—of or related to the second year of high school or college.

varsity—the main team that represents a school in athletic or other competition. Junior varsity is the level below varsity.

ONLINE RESOURCES

**Booklinks
NONFICTION NETWORK**
FREE! ONLINE NONFICTION RESOURCES

To learn more about Tom Brady, please visit **abdobooklinks.com** or scan this QR code. These links are routinely monitored and updated to provide the most current information available.

INDEX

Atlanta Falcons, 22

Baltimore Ravens, 18
baseball, 6, 8, 9
Belichick, Bill, 12
birth, 6
Bledsoe, Drew, 12
Brady, Benjamin, 18
Brady, John, 16
Brady, Vivian, 18
Buffalo Bills, 18
Bündchen, Gisele, 16, 18

California, 6, 8
Carolina Panthers, 14
childhood, 6, 8
COVID-19 pandemic, 24, 26

Deflategate scandal, 20, 22

education, 8, 9, 10

family, 6, 8, 16, 18, 22, 23, 24, 26

health, 18, 20

Indianapolis Colts, 12

Junipero Serra High School, 8

Kansas City Chiefs, 4, 26

leadership, 4
Los Angeles Rams, 24

Mahomes, Patrick, 26
Major League Baseball, 9
Michigan, 9, 10
Montana, Joe, 6, 23
Montreal Expos, 9
Most Valuable Player (MVP), 4, 13, 14, 16, 22, 26
Moynahan, Bridget, 16

National Football League (NFL), 4, 10, 11, 15, 16
New England Patriots, 4, 11, 12, 13, 14, 15, 16, 18, 20, 22, 24

New York Giants, 16, 20
NFL draft, 10, 11

Orange Bowl, 10

Philadelphia Eagles, 14, 24

San Francisco 49ers, 6
St. Louis Rams, 12, 13
Super Bowl, 4, 12, 13, 14, 15, 16, 18, 20, 22, 23, 24, 26

Tampa Bay Buccaneers, 4, 24, 26
TB12 Method, 20

University of Michigan, 9, 10